THIS WALKER BOOK BELONGS TO:

_____

_____

_____

_____

For Rachel and Helen

With special thanks to
Lucy, Helen, David, Amelia and Liz

First published 1995 by Walker Books Ltd
87 Vauxhall Walk, London SE11 5HJ

This edition published 1997

2 4 6 8 10 9 7 5 3 1

This book has been typeset in Horley Old Style.

Printed in Hong Kong

British Library Cataloguing in Publication Data
A catalogue record for this book is
available from the British Library.

ISBN 0-7445-5254-0

Daisy Rabbit's
TREE HOUSE

Penny Dale

WALKER BOOKS
AND SUBSIDIARIES

LONDON • BOSTON • SYDNEY

This is the village of Sandy Edge, which lies beside Lapping Water Lake. All sorts of animals live here, so there are all sorts of houses. On summer days you'll find many animals playing down by the water.

In a lane that winds up from the shore
is the Rabbits' green grassy house. Here are
Mr and Mrs Rabbit, Daisy Rabbit and her
little brother Digger. They live next door to
the Hedgehogs' prickly brown house.

There is a tree house in the Rabbits' back garden.
Here is Daisy Rabbit getting ready to camp out in
it for the night, with her friends Nelly
Jumbo, Deborah Zebra and
Nipper Hedgehog. It is
their favourite thing to do.

Not long ago Daisy felt homesick sleeping any-where but in her own bed. Once she stayed at Nelly Jumbo's house. At first everything was fine. She had a lovely big tea and a splashy bath in the sink.

But at bedtime she felt a bit sad.

She lay in her jumbo hammock and thought

of her own little bed at home, with all her

pictures round it. She didn't say anything,

but she wished she was there instead.

Another time Daisy stayed at Deborah
Zebra's house. At first she had a wonderful
time. They dressed up as fairies and later
they played hide-and-seek
under the table.

But at bedtime Daisy felt sad again.

She looked around at Deborah and all the

little Zebras, and it made her think how much

she missed Digger. She didn't say anything,

but she wished she was with him instead.

Then Daisy stayed at Nipper Hedgehog's house.

At first she was very happy. But at bedtime

she suddenly missed her

mother so much, she couldn't help crying.

The Hedgehogs were very kind to her.

Mr Hedgehog gave her a great big prickly

hedgehog hug and Nipper brought her a drink.

Then Mrs Hedgehog tucked her up gently.

"Sleep well, Daisy," whispered Nipper.

The next day Daisy felt better and when she got home she told her mum everything.

"I don't think I can stay the night with my friends any more," she said.

Mrs Rabbit thought, then she had an idea.

"What if you all slept in the tree house?" she asked.

"Maybe you wouldn't feel homesick there."

So that's what they did. And Daisy didn't
feel homesick a bit. Everyone had tea. Everyone
had baths. Then Daisy, Nelly, Deborah, Nipper
and Digger all snuggled up in the tree house.
Mrs Rabbit read them a story.

"Once upon a time," she began…

And at the end of the story, Mrs Rabbit

turned down the lantern and tiptoed gently

away down the garden.

When she looked back, what did she see?

Five little friends in the soft summer moonlight,

all fast asleep in the tree house.

"Good night," she whispered.

MORE WALKER PAPERBACKS
For You to Enjoy

Also by Penny Dale

TEN IN THE BED

"A subtle variation on the traditional nursery song, illustrated with wonderfully warm pictures ... crammed with amusing details." *Practical Parenting*

0-7445-1340-5   £4.50

TEN OUT OF BED

"A counting backwards version of 'Ten in the Bed'... Penny Dale's warm and distinctive illustrations are full of action and movement ... lots to look at, smile at and talk about." *Children's Books of the Year*

0-7445-4383-5   £4.99

BET YOU CAN'T!

"A lively argumentative dialogue – using simple, repetitive words – between two children. Illustrated with great humour and realism." *Practical Parenting*

0-7445-1225-5   £3.99

ROSIE'S BABIES
written by Martin Waddell

Winner of the Best Book for Babies Award and Shortlisted for the Kate Greenaway Medal.

"Deals with sibling jealousy in a very convincing way." *Child Education*

0-7445-2335-4   £4.50

Walker Paperbacks are available from most booksellers, or by post from B.B.C.S., P.O. Box 941, Hull, North Humberside HU1 3YQ

24 hour telephone credit card line 01482 224626

To order, send: Title, author, ISBN number and price for each book ordered, your full name and address, cheque or postal order payable to BBCS for the total amount and allow the following for postage and packing: UK and BFPO: £1.00 for the first book, and 50p for each additional book to a maximum of £3.50. Overseas and Eire: £2.00 for the first book, £1.00 for the second and 50p for each additional book. Prices and availability are subject to change without notice.